First published in Great Britain 2017 by Walker Books Ltd
87 Vauxhall Walk, London SE11 5HJ

First published in the USA by Disney-Hyperion
British publication rights arranged with Wernick & Pratt Agency, LLC

10 9 8 7 6 5 4 3 2 1

This book has been typeset in MrsEaves

Printed and bound in China

British Library Cataloguing in Publication Data:
a catalogue record for this book is available from the British Library

ISBN 978-1-4063-7369-1

www.walker.co.uk

DiVA
and
FLEA

A PARISIAN TALE

MO WiLLEMS *and*
TONY DiTERLizzi

WALKER
BOOKS

Pour mes amis parisiens

Mo

For Mimi, who is part Diva and part Flea

Tony

Le
DÉBUT

Diva & Flea: THEN

This is Diva's story.

For as long as she could remember, Diva lived at 11 avenue Le Play in Paris, France.

11 avenue Le Play was a grand old apartment building with a small gated courtyard in front. Many people lived in the building: children, parents, old ladies, even an artist or two.

Like most grand old apartment buildings in Paris, there was a *gardienne*, who lived on the ground floor. It was her job to make sure that everything inside and outside the building was neat, tidy and safe.

Diva was the *gardienne*'s dog, which meant that Diva was practically responsible for the whole of 11 avenue Le Play, including the courtyard. It was a very big job for a very small dog.

Diva took her job seriously. Every day she would exit the grand front door, trot across the small courtyard and stand at the building's front gate. From there she watched and guarded, and guarded and watched.

And if anything ever happened, no matter how big or small, Diva would yelp and run away.

Diva was very good at her job.

This is Flea's story.

For as long as he could remember, Flea also lived in Paris, France. But at no fixed address. Flea lived wherever he was, which usually was somewhere different from where it had been the day before.

Flea did not even have a fixed name. Some people called him "Puss" or "Midnight" or "Richard", but he didn't care too much about what people called him. He liked the name "Flea". He thought it was a funny name because he was a large cat, and a flea is a small animal.

Also, he may or may not have had fleas.

Flea did have a fixed occupation, however. He was a *flâneur*. A *flâneur* is someone (or somecat) who wanders the streets and bridges and alleys of the city just to see what there is to see. A great *flâneur* has seen everything but

still looks for more, because there is always
more to discover.

Flea was a really great *flâneur*.

2

The Courtyard

One afternoon, Flea was having a particularly good time *flâneur*ing. The day was barely half over, and he had already discovered a staircase that led deep under the streets of Paris. There, giant rooms on wheels would suddenly appear and release large groups of people.

So, thought Flea, that's where people come from.

Later, Flea found himself sitting in the sun watching people who were also sitting in the sun watching even more people sitting in the sun. Everyone except for Flea was drinking tiny cups of something they called Cough-Fee. (This is pretty much what people do in Paris, France.)

Then, inside Flea's favourite shop, he saw a woman drop a giant piece of salami smack onto the floor. Flea pounced and snatched the salami before the Man with the Broom could even chase him out (an event that was both unusual and delicious).

And, if that weren't enough, that very same day Flea happened to wander past the courtyard at 11 avenue Le Play, where he saw Diva for the first time.

As soon as Flea saw the small dog, he was captivated. As soon as Diva saw the large cat,

she yelped and ran away.

Flea laughed, because it was kind of funny. (He had seen many funny things in his life, but he had never seen such a small dog yelp with such a loud voice.)

After that, Flea would make sure that most afternoons he just happened to *flâneur* right by the courtyard of 11 avenue Le Play. It was fun watching the small dog yelp and run away.

This went on for many days. Flea would *flâneur* by, the small dog would yelp and run away, Flea would laugh. It was almost too good to be true.

Then one day Diva didn't yelp or run away. Instead, she looked right at Flea's big face and asked, "Are you *trying* to hurt my feelings?"

Flea had never thought about it like that.

3

The Mouse

The next day, Diva trotted into the courtyard expecting to see the large cat and to hear his loud laugh.

But the cat was not there. It was quiet.

Diva was surprised at how empty the courtyard felt without a cat sticking his big head through the gate.

Then she noticed that the courtyard wasn't completely empty. There was a small dead

mouse near the front step.

Diva looked at the mouse and thought for a moment. Then she called out as loudly as she could, "WHO LEFT THIS MOUSE BY MY DOORSTEP?!"

A small voice hiding in the bushes replied, "Me."

It was Flea's voice. Diva was surprised a cat that big could have a voice that small.

The cat came out from behind the bushes and walked to the edge of the gate. "I did not mean to hurt your feelings," he said. "So I brought you a mouse."

"You brought me a mouse?" asked Diva.

"To show you how sorry I am," he replied.

Diva looked at the mouse and thought for a moment. Then she walked over to Flea and said, "That is the nicest thing anyone has ever done for me. But in the future, bring me a small piece of ribbon, OK?"

Flea laughed. And this time, so did Diva.

Le
PREMIER
ENTRACTE

4

Feet!

After Diva and Flea had shared their first laugh together, Diva invited Flea to visit her courtyard every day.

Diva would stand by the gate as Flea told stories about The Underground Rooms on Wheels, The People Who Drink Cough-Fee All Day, The Piece of Salami and the Broom that Missed, and more of his many adventures.

Diva had never thought about the world beyond her courtyard before she heard Flea's amazing stories. She especially liked the one about the tower so tall and so pointy that it could cut a cloud in half, like a knife slicing through a soft piece of delicious cheese.

Diva loved cheese.

For Diva, just inside her courtyard gate was the most wonderful place on earth for listening to Flea's stories. There, the sun warmed her fur and his stories warmed her imagination.

But then, as often as not, she would

hear the ominous *click-clack*ing of feet either entering or exiting the apartment building. Diva was a small dog, smaller than a person's foot. The way a foot tended to come crashing down from the sky made her aware of just how *squishable* she was.

The fact that feet usually travelled in pairs did not help things one bit.

As soon as she heard the telltale *click-clack*ing, Diva would yell "FEET!" and run away.

After enough time had passed, Diva would slowly return to the courtyard.

Then Flea could resume his story. That is, until that telltale *click-clack*ing returned. Diva couldn't help but yell "FEET!" and run away again. It was who she was.

"I like telling you my stories," Flea told Diva with a smile, "but they sure take a long time to finish."

5

A Big Thought

*O*ne day, after he had *finally* told the story of The Shop Where the Man Roasts Whole Chickens and Could Learn a Thing or Two About Sharing, Flea said, "Well, time for me to go."

"Where will you go when you go?" asked Diva curiously.

"Where *won't* I go when I go where I go!" replied Flea proudly.

"How am I supposed to know where you *won't* go when you go, when I don't know where you *do* go when you go?" asked Diva.

By now, their little-dog and big-cat brains were very confused.

Unsure of what to do next, Diva thought of yelling "FEET!" and running away, but there were no feet anywhere to be seen. So Diva just stood there.

"You should join me one day!" said Flea suddenly. "You could be a *flâneur*, like me."

"What is a *flâneur*?" asked Diva, worried that it might be a type of mouse catcher.

Flea explained that a *flâneur* is someone (or somecat, or maybe even somedog) who wanders the streets and bridges and alleys of the city just to see what there is to see. And a great *flâneur* has seen everything but still looks for more, because there is always more to discover.

"I am a great *flâneur*," Flea said with his tail raised high. "That is how I discovered you."

"But little dogs like me are not *flâneurs*," said Diva certainly.

"There are always exceptions," replied Flea. "They are what make you exceptional."

Diva thought about being a *flâneur*. Simply imagining the big buildings and the giant parks and the wide avenues and the tower that could cut a cloud in half made her shiver.

The world was larger than she had thought possible, and it was all right there, on the other side of the courtyard gate.

That was a big thought for a little dog.

6

A Big Step

*D*iva had spent the whole night thinking about the big thought from the day before. So in the morning she was tired and impatient for Flea to arrive from his early *flâneur*ing.

"I have been thinking," said Diva before Flea could poke his head through the courtyard gate. "I have been thinking about becoming a *flâneur*, like you."

"Excellent!" purred Flea. "Let's go!"

"Now?" asked Diva.

"A *flâneur* does not need a plan to have an adventure," said Flea. "A *flâneur* creates an adventure whenever the opportunity arises."

"Oh," said Diva quietly. Even though she had spent the whole night thinking, she had not thought of that.

"I can show you the giant tower that can cut a cloud in half," said Flea unexpectedly. "It is just around the corner."

"Around the corner?" gulped Diva. She also hadn't thought she would have to travel *that* far.

"Come on!" said Flea as he turned and dashed onto the pavement.

Diva did not move.

Flea looked at her from the middle of the pavement and smiled a gentle smile. "Take a

little step and see how it feels," he said.

Even a little step felt like a big step to Diva. The pavement was large and different and very not courtyardy. But if Flea was there (and he was), then it couldn't be all that bad.

So, slowly and carefully, Diva scrunched her nose and followed in Flea's pawsteps. She passed through the courtyard gate for the first time ever, leaving behind the place where she had lived her whole entire life.

It took her many steps to reach Flea on the pavement, but eventually she did.

"Isn't this fun?" asked Flea.

Diva did not think it was fun; but it was … exceptional.

7

The Corner

Diva could not believe she was with Flea on the pavement. The world looked very different from all the way out here. She could even see her apartment building!

"This is really something," Diva said excitedly. "Do you see me? I'm *flâneuring*!"

"We haven't finished yet," said Flea before dashing around the corner and completely disappearing.

Diva gasped. There she was, alone, outside, in the middle of the pavement, by herself, without anyone else. In one direction was her home. In the other direction was her friend.

Diva took a deep breath.

She scrunched her nose tight.

She took a step towards the corner.

Step by little step, Diva reached the corner. Then she turned and saw something wondrous.

In front of her stood a giant steel tower, completely different from how she had imagined yet just as Flea had described it: big and strong and gentle and delicate all at the same time. It was so beautiful; Diva felt both smaller and larger just being in its presence.

A tower that amazing makes people stop and stare. A tower that tremendous makes people from all over the world come just to see it. Lots and lots and LOTS of people. Lots and lots and lots of people with lots and lots of ...

"FEET!"

I am not a great *flâneur* yet, said Diva to herself a few seconds later, safe inside the apartment building at 11 avenue Le Play.

But I am brave.

Le DEUXIÈME ENTRACTE

8

A Strange Noise

Flea surprised Diva by arriving outside the courtyard gate first thing the next morning. He was eager to discuss The Adventure of the Tower Around the Corner.

Diva thought she had been very brave. Flea wasn't sure Diva had been as brave as she thought she had been. But then again, as Diva pointed out, Flea hadn't tried something new the day before.

Suddenly Flea became very quiet.

"I did not mean to hurt your feelings," said Diva.

"It's not that," replied Flea. He had heard a strange noise from inside the building. It sounded like *Krrrr-WHOOSH-krrrr-FOOF!* or maybe it sounded like *Krrrr-FOOF-krrrr-WHOOSH!*

Flea wanted to know what that sound was.
"Oh," said Diva simply, "that's breakfast."
"Breck-Fest?" asked Flea, sounding out
the word for the first time. This was exciting;
Flea was discovering a new thing.

He pondered for a second. Then he asked, with a touch of jealousy, "Is Breck-Fest your friend?"

"Kind of," replied Diva with a laugh. "Come and see!"

Suddenly Diva ran through the doorway into 11 avenue Le Play. She looked at Flea from inside and smiled a kind smile. "Take a little step and see how it feels," she said.

"Very funny," replied Flea. But he did not move.

"Are you coming?" Diva asked.

"I am a *flâneur*," Flea said. "Of course I am coming."

But still he did not move.

9
A Grand Sight

Flea was a great *flâneur*, but he was no fool. He knew there were many surprises inside buildings, some of which included brooms. The fact that brooms usually swung at visiting cats did not help things one bit.

But if Diva was inside (and she was), it couldn't be that bad. So, slowly and carefully, he followed in Diva's pawsteps.

Flea had seen many things, and yet his tail shot up when he saw the grand entrance hall. There were giant mirrors in golden frames, fancy designs carved on the stone walls, and a marble floor that made Diva's toenails click as she walked across it.

There was also an open door. "That is where I live," said Diva before dashing through the doorway and completely disappearing.

Flea took a deep breath and said, "It is a good thing I am so brave." But he did not say it very loudly. Then he crept towards the door.

Behind the door was an apartment with a table and chairs and a wall covered with photographs of Diva sitting, smiling and running away from things. The photographs were all different except for one thing: Diva looked happy in all of them.

Flea realized that someone must stop and look at these photographs often and smile, just like he was smiling now.

Then he realized that no one had ever bothered to take a picture of him.

That was a big thought for Flea. Big enough for him to forget where he was for a second.

Flea turned to Diva to ask her about the photographs, and noticed that she was sitting right next to a pair of feet. And that pair of feet was right next to a—

"BROOM!" yelled Flea. "RUN AWAY, DIVA! RUN AWAY!"

10

A Little Bit Magic

lea took his own advice. He ran as fast as he could out of the apartment, across the entrance hall, past the doorway, through the courtyard, around the gate and on to the safety of the big, wide pavement outside.

But Diva did not follow him.

Flea was not sure what to do. He was here, and Diva was there. Did Diva need rescuing? If so, Flea knew he was the only cat between

Diva, a pair of feet and a broom.

So Flea returned. Inside, he saw Diva still sitting and smiling right next to the pair of feet and the broom.

Wow, thought Flea. Diva really is brave.

Suddenly the feet began to move.

Suddenly the *broom* began to move!

Flea's eyes grew wide. But the broom did not swing at him. Instead it began to swish back and forth in a kind of *sweeping* motion — as if it wasn't concerned about Flea in the least.

"Don't worry about *that* broom," said Diva calmly. "That is a nice broom. It belongs to Eva. She's the *gardienne*, and she lives here with me."

Flea had no idea what a *gardienne* was, but he was pretty sure Eva was a human-type person. Flea had seen people and dogs take walks together in the park, but he never imagined

that they could *live* together. Everything inside
this apartment was so ... odd.

"Let me show you something," said Diva
as she walked right past Eva's feet and the
sweeping broom. Flea bravely followed her to
a corner, where he saw a bowl filled with ...
something.

"This," Diva said happily, "is breakfast."

At first Flea was disappointed. Diva's

friend did not seem very interesting. Then he
noticed a particularly delicious smell.

"Food," he said. "It's FOOD!" Food was
his very favourite thing — next to Diva, that is.

"Have some," invited Diva.

Flea had eaten food in the morning
before, but he had never seen food just sitting
there *waiting* to be eaten. He took a big bite,
and then another, and then another, without

ever once looking over his shoulder or having to quickly scamper away.

"The inside of 11 avenue Le Play may be weird," said Flea with a mouthful of Breck-Fest, "but it is also a little bit magic."

La
FIN

11

A Favour

The very first thing the next day, Flea rushed to 11 avenue Le Play in the hope that Breck-Fest was more than a once-in-a-lifetime thing. Luckily, Breck-Fest happened with great regularity in Diva's apartment.

After their meal, Diva and Flea sat in a patch of warm sunlight in the middle of the courtyard. Curious, Flea asked Diva, "Why are you afraid of the feet out here but not afraid of the feet inside?"

"The feet inside end in Eva," said Diva. "But I don't know *what* is at the end of the feet out here."

Diva's answer gave Flea an idea, and it was such an exciting idea that his tail shot straight up. Flea turned to his friend. "You showed me a wondrous and delicious new thing yesterday. I owe you a favour."

Diva was flattered. Also, she loved favours.

"What is the favour?" she asked, hoping it would be a piece of ribbon and not another dead mouse.

"I will show you how to meet new feet," said Flea.

This was not Diva's idea of a favour, but Flea was insistent. "It will be a wondrous thing," he said.

Diva did not say anything.

"I will be right here by your side the whole time," continued Flea. "Trust me."

Diva looked at Flea. "OK," she said. But she did not say it very loudly.

Suddenly Diva and Flea heard the telltale *click-clack*ing sounds of strange footsteps coming from the street.

"Feet!" whispered Diva nervously. Every part of her wanted to turn and run away. Every part, that is, except the part that trusted Flea.

So Diva stayed.

Diva waited.

Diva trusted.

12

Feet, Again

*C*lick–clack! *Clack–click! Click–CLACK!* Diva could hear the feet coming closer. Then she could *see* the feet coming closer. Flea did not move. So Diva did not move either.

Then the feet came to a stop right in front of Diva!

"Say 'Miaow'," instructed Flea.

"Woof!" said Diva.

"Close enough," said Flea.

The almost-miaow must have done something, because just then a huge hand, almost as large as a foot, appeared out of the sky.

Diva looked at Flea. Flea whispered, "The wondrous thing is coming." Diva scrunched up her nose and closed her eyes, but still she did not move. Then the hand touched Diva's head and started to pet it!

The hand was gentle and friendly. If it could have talked, it would have said something like, "Why, hello there. You are very nice, and I am very glad that we can share this moment. You have made my day a little better, and I hope I have made your day a little better too."

Wow, thought Diva, that was a *wondrous* favour.

"Told you," said Flea. "Now, what was that thing you were saying about something called Luh-Unch?"

13

Diva & Flea:
NOW

*T*his is Diva now.

Diva lives with Eva, the *gardienne* of 11 avenue Le Play in Paris, France. Sometimes she and her friend, a big cat named Flea, pass through the courtyard gate to discover new things and meet new feet on the streets and avenues of the city.

Diva has become a *flâneur*, a small dog in a big city who has seen things and done things that other small dogs in Paris have only heard about from passing cats.

Even though Diva has lived many adventures, she still loves stories, especially Flea's.

This is Flea now.

Flea is a great *flâneur* who has seen everything but still looks for more, because there is always more to discover. And now, thanks to his friend, a little dog called Diva, he has discovered that "more" in a most surprising place. It is located through a door that leads to a small apartment in 11 avenue Le Play in Paris, France, which has ample food and ample love. And one harmless broom.

This is where Flea now lives with Diva and Eva. This is where he eats "Breck-Fest" every day. This is where the wall has a photograph of him. These are all parts of his very favourite story; the story he calls The Adventure of When I Found a Friend and a Home at the Same Time.

Au
REVOIR

AUTHOR'S NOTE

For as long as I can remember, I've wanted to live in Paris, France. So one day I decided to do just that. I flew to Paris, looked around and found an apartment in a grand old building with a small, gated courtyard. Like many grand old apartment buildings in Paris, this building had a *gardienne*. She was a nice lady with a nice dog.

The dog was very small, smaller than one of my feet. But she was brave and friendly. She let me pet her, and when I did, it almost sounded like she was purring.

The *gardienne* asked me why I had moved to Paris. I told her that I was a writer and I was looking for a story to write about. I hoped to find a story by wandering all over the streets and bridges of the city, like a *flâneur*.

The small dog barked.

Then the *gardienne* told me something amazing. She said she would introduce me to a famous *flâneur* that very day!

"Really?" I asked, surprised that *flâneurs* were so easy to meet.

"Sure," she explained as she scooped up her little dog. "Diva here is best friends with the neighbourhood's most famous *flâneur*."

And that's when the cat came in.

So I'd found my story before I had even stepped out of my new home. And when I discovered that, I knew that Tony DiTerlizzi was the only artist who could help me tell it.

Mo Willems

Note: Some names and places in this story have been altered to protect the privacy of the animals involved.

ILLUSTRATOR'S NOTE

For as long as I can remember, I have wanted to visit Paris, France. From the famous paintings hanging in the Louvre museum to the perched gargoyles of Notre Dame cathedral watching over the bustling city below, I've dreamed of standing in the presence of the many inspirations that have shaped me as an artist.

I have so many stories buzzing in my head that I hope I can share them all before I forget them. But from time to time, I like to wander off my career path (like a *flâneur*) and experience something unexpected — like a story that I would not have created on my own. So I thank Mo for letting me tag along on his latest literary excursion.

Tony DiTerlizzi

MO WILLEMS, a *New York Times* number one bestselling author and illustrator, has been awarded a Caldecott Honor on three occasions, for *Don't Let the Pigeon Drive the Bus!*, *Knuffle Bunny: A Cautionary Tale* and *Knuffle Bunny Too: A Case of Mistaken Identity*. His celebrated Elephant & Piggie series has won two Theodor Seuss Geisel Medals and five Geisel Honors. Mo began his career as a writer and animator on *Sesame Street*, where he garnered six Emmy Awards. He lives with his family in Massachusetts, not far from his friend Tony DiTerlizzi.

TONY DiTERLIZZI, a *New York Times* number one bestselling author and illustrator, created the middle-grade series *The Spiderwick Chronicles* with Holly Black, which has sold millions of copies, been translated into more than 30 languages and made into a feature film. He won a Caldecott Honor for illustrating *The Spider and the Fly*, and teamed up with Lucasfilm to retell the original Star Wars trilogy in a picture book featuring artwork by Academy Award-winning concept artist Ralph McQuarrie. Tony lives in Amherst, Massachusetts, with his wife, daughter and dog, Mimi.